The Flight
of the
Animals

Story and Pictures by
Claudine

Parents' Magazine Press / New York

For Alexandra, Peter, Kyra, and Raphael

Not far from the Bay of Bengal, in the green and
tangled jungles of India, there lived a small
short-eared rabbit. This creature was so fearful that
even the sight of his own shadow could make him
tremble. So he seldom left his burrow, going out only
at night to search for a bit of food.
One day, feeling a little braver than usual, he poked
his nose out, and seeing that it was a nice day
he decided to stretch out in the sun near a tall carob
tree. Carefully he looked to the right and the left,
but there was no sign of an enemy. So he quickly hopped
to the spot he had chosen, and he settled down for
a rest in the warm sunlight.

As he lay there, he studied the dense leaves of the carob tree, and he saw the ripening brown seed pods hanging from the branches. "Ah," he thought to himself, "soon they will fall to the ground and I will be able to eat their honey sweetness."

Then suddenly, an alarming thought came to this foolish rabbit. What would happen if the earth should begin to cave in? Where would he go for safety? The more he thought of it the more terrified he became until his heart was ready to burst from fear.

And just at that moment some playful monkeys in a
nearby palm tree let drop a heavy ripe coconut. With a
thundering crash it landed on the ground behind the
rabbit. In a panic he leapt to his feet and scampered
off as fast as his legs would carry him.

As he ran he passed a long-eared hare. "Why are you
running so fast?" asked the hare. "Are you having a race
with the wind?"

But the rabbit didn't dare to pause long enough to give
an answer.
Now the hare was more curious than ever to know
the reason for the rabbit's flight. So he ran
beside him and again asked the question. The fleeing
rabbit just managed to pant out, "The earth is
caving in behind us!"
The hare was just as frightened to hear this as the
rabbit had been when he heard the crash of the coconut,
and he raced along to flee from the disaster. One
by one they were joined by other rabbits and hares until
there were hundreds of them racing through the jungle.

A doe and a deer standing in a clump of banyan trees
were startled to see this horde come racing past.
But when they learned that the earth was caving in,
without hesitation they joined the rabbits and hares.
Presently they came upon a huge rhinoceros, and in
no time at all he was lumbering along with the rest.

And before long the stampede included bears and
elks, wild oxen and gnus, jackals, monkeys, tapirs,
camels, leopards, and even elephants. At this point,
a young tiger saw the fleeing animals, and mounting
a large rock he roared three times. The thunder
of his roar was so great the whole valley shook.
The animals stopped in their tracks, for fearful
as they were about the earth caving in, they feared
the voice of their king even more.

"Why are you all running like this?" he demanded
to know.

With one voice they answered, "The earth is caving in
behind us and we must seek safety."

"Who saw it caving in?" asked the tiger.

"Ask the leopards. They know," replied the elephants.

"We didn't see it," said the leopards, "but the wild
boars told us so."

And the wild boars answered, "Oh, we didn't see it
either, but the camels know all about it."

And the camels pointed to the tapirs who pointed to the
deer who pointed to the hares who pointed to the rabbits.

One by one the tiger patiently questioned the rabbits
until he came at last to the short-eared rabbit
who had started it all.

"Are you the one who saw the earth cave in?" asked the
tiger, and he fixed his fierce eyes upon the little rabbit.

The poor creature was even more terrified than before,
but he managed to stutter, "Y-yes, Your Ma-majesty."

"Where did you see this happen?" the tiger continued.

"Near my home, in a grove of coconut palms and carob trees. I was lying there in the sun, thinking of what would happen to me if the earth suddenly began to cave in. Just then I heard the crash of the earth breaking up right behind me, and I fled."

"Come," said the tiger in a gentler voice. "Show me the spot where you heard the earth breaking up."

"Your Majesty, I am afraid to go near that spot," said the rabbit. "By now it must surely be no more than a great hole."

"Do not fear anything when you are with me," replied the tiger. "Hop on my back and I will carry you there."

Together they returned to the spot where the rabbit
had basked in the sun. And there, upon the palm fronds
on the ground, the tiger found the coconut that had
fallen and frightened the rabbit.
"It is better, little one," said the tiger, "that you
speak not at all if you speak without knowledge.
Now let us return to the other animals."

And to them he said, before he sent them back to their homes, "Believe not everything you hear. If I had not stopped you in time, surely you all would have hurled yourselves into the Bay of Bengal and perished by now."